Stranger in You

Selected Poems
& New

MARY DI MICHELE

Toronto
Oxford University Press
1995

Oxford University Press
70 Wynford Drive, Don Mills, Ontario M3C 1J9

Oxford New York
Athens Auckland Bangkok Bombay
Calcutta Cape Town Dar es Salaam Delhi
Florence Hong Kong Istanbul Karachi
Kuala Lumpur Madras Madrid Melbourne
Mexico City Nairobi Paris Singapore
Taipei Tokyo Toronto

and associated companies in
Berlin Ibadan

Oxford is a trademark of Oxford University Press

Many of the poems have been edited and changed, tinkered with, not major revisions, because I have tried at the same time to honour the vision of the younger poet who wrote them. Some acknowledgements are required for the new poems, *Matrix* for the 'My Hart Crane' poems and the anthology *Because You Were A Stranger* for 'Fragment of Blue' dedicated to Patrick Lane on his 55th birthday. For continuing support and thoughtful readings and comments on the poems I'd like to thank Kim Maltman, Roo Borson, Russell Brown and my daughter Emily Newson. Special thanks to Erin Mouré for advice on the making of a selected poems, to Esther Dragonieri for the cover image, and to Cameron Hayne for the author photo.

Canadian Cataloguing in Publication Data
Di Michele, Mary, 1949–
    Stranger in you: selected poems & new

ISBN 0-19-541158-7

I. Title

PS8557.I55S87 1995   C811'.54   C95-931936-0
PR9199.3.D55S87 1995

CONTENTS

for my mother and father
Concetta and Vincenzo di Michele

By recognizing *our* uncanny strangeness we shall
neither suffer from it nor enjoy it from the outside.
The foreigner is within me, hence we are all
foreigners.

Julia Kristeva

We write, we paint, throughout our entire lives as
if we were going to a foreign country, as if we were
foreigners inside our own families.

Hélène Cixous

BORN IN AUGUST

Born in the fifth house
under the sign of Leo
on the sixth of August,
four years after Hiroshima,
180 years after the birth
of Napoleon Bonaparte,
born Maria Luisa di Michele,
baptized at Santa Lucia
in an ancient town, Lanciano,
of the single miracle, since the middle
ages, the host, bleeding for you.
Born in the wake of World War Two,
in the green, though scarred, hills of Abruzzo
where the Allied guns and the German guns
rendevoused. All I knew of this history were family
anecdotes yet for years I dreamt of low flying
planes overhead, dropping their exploding cargo.
Austerlitz, Auschwitz, Hiroshima!
Born with the rising sun,
the predator moon, a lion,
born from a woman's will to survive
the concentration camp, to continue
in awe to see again the blue
eyes of the dead. When she cradled
her first child, she recognized
her father looking up from her arms.
And so my mother lost her teeth
while I grew minature bones
like pearls in an oyster mouth.

A STRANGE GRACE
for my grandmother

Love always dressed herself in black.
She was a fat old woman with dark eyes.
Love always loved me best,
her golden grandchild, the one
who tried to explain herself
right into her heart
for a little chocolate cheese
gilded in foil.

She was an octogenarian, love, a matriarch,
and her heart tracked for light
years in its slow orbit in the space
of the chest. Love knew the ivory
limit of her universe and the miracle
of a child emerging with the first light,
in chiaroscuro on the horizon, a cry
drawn out of the nurturing darkness,
a free fall with a strange grace toward another
kind of darkness,

and the precocious day chattering and chattering,
as if she couldn't shut up for a second,
as if she couldn't shut up for good,
as if the world could just keep busy on the tip
of her tongue.

Love always dressed herself in black.
Posing with her, seated on a white marble bench
by the Roman gardens, as I stood on the stone slab
our heads were level, the silver and the gold.
My crescent arm around her neck
embracing a primordial passion,
deeper than forests of Brazilian cocoa,
my truest, my dearest love, in the whole of time,
in the intimacy of my innocence,

the love I left for a new world,
far away from her old country seat,

sealed in marble and invisible
love, who always loved me best.

WAITING FOR *BABBO*

The year was a chasm gaping.
I lost some heart in that darkness.
I lost my father for the first time
to the sea, to *america*.

The year is a desert canyon
stretching beyond the arid horizon
where the dust dreams of breathing
through gills in water. I dream
of seeing my father again in the wide
black and white screens of *america*.

I am four, a year to you, *babbo*,
is twenty to me, twenty years
and I am five, I have grown old
without you. I have dressed as a gypsy
for *Carnevale*. The sacrifice in the bonfire
was my rocking horse for the end of winter.
In a few days, *babbo*, we pack
the smiles that are destined for you.

But if a year is twenty, twenty
years lost in snow is an ice
age. Can it be redeemed
by an olive branch or a palm?
And that dark skeleton
waiting is not my father.

CARA

The hand-coloured darling in the black
and white photograph is me, acquiring
the look of an antique. I am
propped up on the table, I am

a feast for your eyes.To be beautiful
at three was not difficult. To be diffident.
To be blessed with hair of soft spun
honey and eyes of lapis lazuli, to be

initiated into the tricks of the vanity so young.
This is the picture which dreams itself larger
than my life. (Half-ashamed) my parents display it,
the photo, proof, the photo serving both as shrine

and trophy, mounted like the stuffed head
of a fawn accidentally killed in a hunt.

ENIGMATICO

His limpid skin is green gold as he reclines
in a shade that crowns him with the leaves
of vines. As smooth as the golden skinned
grapes his thighs are about to burst their denim
husks, the golden thighs of a man of bronze.

Eyes of pale amber, with the bite of brandy.
Lips that kiss her lady's shoe, her knee,
the liquid outward curve of her hip,
lips that call her madonna!
his dream of a bright aproned
jewel for his kitchen,
he polishes it there in the long grass of August
until he rips her leisurely as a silk,
and she cries out caught

4

with one bare foot in a village in Abruzzo,
the other laced into English shoes in Toronto,
she strides the Atlantic legs stretched
like a Colossus.

Photograph of a girl dressed as a gypsy,
child waist pinched by a red girdle,
for *Carnevale*,

in another world, wearing the black academic gown,
a rabbit skin around her shoulders,
she hangs on the wall of a suburban bungalow.

HOW TO KILL YOUR FATHER

He breaks a promise on the road to Firenze.
You will not speak to him all through
the drive in the Tuscan hills,
the rented Alpha Romeo bitches
but the poplar's got your tongue,
long and green and aloof.

You abandon the car and walk
into a Roman afternoon.
You know how to kill your father,
he knows how to kill you.

The sky is waving white cloud
kerchiefs to wipe away your tears,
to offer a truce, if not the truth
in the family. In the intensifying heat
even the wind begins to wilt, its wings
of feather and wax melting.

You are alone on the highway to the sun.
Your North American education

has taught you how to kill a father
but you are walking down an Italian

via, so you will surrender
and visit him in the hospital
where you will be accused
of wishing his death
in wanting a life
for yourself.

A scorpion's sting darkening
your heart buries July in Italy.

BENVENUTO

The same chickens are scratching in the yard,
the same light is making tracks across the hills,
the same wind is beating its head against the stucco
walls of the houses in the village,
as evening settles into itself,
the light pulling up its seat in the valley
and tucking its legs under it.

Twenty years and my Canadian feet formed of prairie wheat
can still find their own way, can run ahead
while my thoughts seem to resist and find
the pomegranate, the fig and the olive
trees of my grandmother's orchard, in the back of a house
tucked into the pocket of a hill, leaning into it
with the declining light. I stop under a pomegranate tree,
a favourite retreat, under the ripening fruit,
old dreams are pricking at the back of my mind.
I tear one open to eat and it recognizes me
with *benvenuto* in all its myriad, ruby eyes.

THE DISGRACE

ma una sola vergogna non ci ha mai toccato,
non saremo mai donne, mai ombre a nessuno.
                                    Cesare Pavese

A skinned rabbit sits in a bowl of blood.
In the foetal position, it dreams its own death.
I swell quietly by the warmth of the kitchen,
like the yolk that is the hidden sun in the egg.

The old wives and the new wives are
chattering, the intimate news of an idle
moment. Their children are blowing
like seedclocks in the yard, they are
safe for now. The girls are ready to
fling themselves, rejoicing in spring
breezes, transported by *splendor*
in the grass. Some of the boys will surely

jump the fence. On the first day I forget
to play. Curled up with cramps in the corner,
I am one among the snails climbing the wall
by the stove, the stew pot heating below,
trying to sip camomile tea, with a blanket
wrapped around my middle to ease the first

labour of blood. My mother and aunts
serve the unwritten stories of their lives
which they wipe away without pause
to reflect and the crumbs on the table.

They all dine on rabbit stew and the snails
are antipasto, good wives, good women, the best cooks,
and wash the many courses down with an inch of red
wine in their glasses and the carafe brimming with
unspoken desire. This blood is anonymous
and at times gives off such a strong odour

7

that lettuce wilts in the hand
and new wine turns sour
and onions cry in their sleeves.

My blood is knotted into worry
beads. Deliver me, if you can,
from the cup that I am,
the spilling cup.

The ladies, *le signore*, are ready to repeat
stories as my mother offers coffee and cake.
Ti ricordi, zio Gianni, who made his wife suffer,
the poor saint, bringing in his mistress to live
with the family, her own room, for the slut,
while the wife was made to play
the servant; he sent the children to school
with *biscotti* in their lunches, such a treat,
when their lips were so firmly sealed from
shame they could not eat or speak;

Maria Luisa, my father's youngest sister,
went mad it seemed in her sleep
she tried to kill the elder, Chiarina,
with a knife then slit her own throat
in the hospital a week later and I'm named
after her, the consequences to be revealed

by the stars, while Giuliano, my brother, was
named in the spirit of a good joke by my father
after a Sicilian bandit, hung on his birthday;
my mother didn't laugh then, but she smiles
today because her son has sidestepped
this curse and works with computers in
accounting, as she tells the anecdote, cutting
another piece of cake, pouring
another cup of coffee,

Filomena, whose husband was sent to Ethiopia
by Mussolini to provide a repast for crocodiles;
stays married to his death, to the unrecoverable
body of love, to yearning as for an eucharist.

And finally, of most recent interest, her daughter,
Anna's wedding night and the sacred mysteries
of a man's sanctified appetite for the blood
he may claim as his own.

I am marking this day of my first
bleeding in red pencil in my work book.
It's a Hilroy Mammoth, the paper is cheap
and would absorb and blot my writing if I used ink.
I am ten years old in Miss Hennessy/Mrs Sullivan's
grade five class at St Thomas Aquinas School.
I like drama. They say I can act but in the choir
they won't let me sing. I just move my lips,
my song is silence. I am only ten years old
but my family is already plotting a different
and disquieting role for me.

Here is my initiation into the confessional of the kitchen
(will that stop my thinking?)
The men are in another room drinking grappa, smoking
cigarettes, while the soccer game roars from the TV.

Through the open doorway I can barely see
the shadows of the men's heads. They think
they are creating life in the living-room
while the dust of the outside world
clings to their shoes, but even men,
when they are common, men
of the trades: barber, plumber, electrician,
who make the real world because they
construct it, do not write their own histories.
They tell similar stories as the women
but as authorities, not as gossips,

with the weight of the fist and the wail
of the accordion. Still they are not featured
in books I read these family Joes.

MIMOSA

I PROLOGUE

Even more than a tired man, Vitto is a sad man,
all Sunday afternoon finds him rocking
in the Brighton rocker, in the backyard
of the house he's earned, under the sky he's
created of green fibreglass, jutting from the roof.
There is only one heaven, the heaven of the home.
There was only one paradise, the garden
that kept them little children even as adults,
until one angel, Lucia, his luckless offspring,
fell, refusing to share in this light.

Sentimental music is being sucked up
from the stereo system in the basement
like a sweet gaseous soda through a straw.
He listens to an Italian tenor sing 'Mimosa'
and savours a bittersweet banishment, a ginger
nostalgia, Canada Dry fizzing in his glass.

Summer's finished. The few roses remaining
are such a dark red you imagine the odour
of menstrual blood. There's a path of broken
tiles through the well trimmed grass leading
to a vegetable patch, fenced and carefully tended,
a nursery for deep purple eggplant, whose mature
passions keep them close to the earth, garlic,
the most eloquent of plants, with the grace of a lily,
from white clusters of buds, as if ironically,
the flower, sticks out its long green tongue. Zucchini,
tomatoes, peppers, tender peas, and Italian parsley,

the season yields. He tries to improve the English of night
classes for new Canadians by reading the daily papers.
Unlike his wife, he can talk to his children in the language
in which they dream, but he keeps that tongue
like a poorly cut key with which he must struggle
to enter alone. He keeps his love
for them like old clothes he no longer wears in public,
though they fit better than his skin. He wants
his girls never to grow up. He wants
Lucia to be three again and dozing in his arms.

His latest project was a hut for storing seeds and tools,
and now there's nothing left
to build a life —
time of development, of homes under construction,
there's nothing left
to be done. The man's hands are idle.
Without brick they brood.

The years spent working in a stone quarry just outside
Toronto taught him how to find the fault
in rock, how to split the pink and white limestone
into slabs. He put a new face on our old
house of fake red brick tarred onto stucco.
But the lines of fracture in his own life stayed hidden,
while working overtime and Saturdays
and what few hours not sold were snored away
in front of the television. This accounted for the distance
he hadn't bargained for as he crossed the Atlantic,
this estrangement from his own children. His good
wife, he didn't have to feel anything for, she worked
hard and cooked well. He might have finished
school, but he married young, just after
the war and hard times made him stop thinking
about himself and dream only for his children.
He doesn't even regret having no son because
his daughters are rare, intelligent and full
of music. Still he's not happy, he's getting old

and Lucia abandoned the family to live in an apartment
on her own. He has no hope
of finding another youth in grandchildren
soon enough. How can he rest when he knows
he'll die sooner than he cares to? He dreads
a fate like his own father's, the left side of his body
paralyzed from a stroke and how he cursed:
'I'll only have to close one eye when I die,
poor you, who'll have to close two.'
Vitto doesn't sleep well but he's learned to
dream with his eyes open.

The voice of the Italian tenor is wailing
'Mimosa' and the moon which is american.
Vitto listens and holds back tears. He remembers
his choice was a poor man's: to starve shooting
off fireworks to celebrate saints' days, in Italy,
in the family trade, working as he worked as a child,
barefoot until he was thirteen and hungry
or to make his way in a new world without mimosa,
where he didn't have to tip his hat to Don So-and-So
for a pittance, where he hoped a man would be judged
by his work and paid for his labour. The good life,
a house and money in the bank, a pension, turned out
not so well without fruitful daughters, his favourite
Lucia makes herself scarce while the other
ressembles her mother.

II MARTA'S MONOLOGUE

All my life I've tried to please my father.
I live at home, teach school around the corner
at St Mary's. I make a good salary and help
children to learn to read and write. I have very
little experience, that's true, but I know enough
to risk nothing, to live where it's safe,
to have a job that's secure, to love those
who love me, my parents, and to offer

the proper respect to our relatives so that
when my uncles gather with my father
around the table I listen very carefully
to all their bullshit as they split *lupini*
throwing the shells into the bowl
I don't fail to serve them.

My elder sister, Lucia, is not like me,
she's not good. She's the first born,
the stubborn one, who wears Italia
like a cheap necklace around her throat,
with a charm that renders her heart green
with tarnish, Lucia, the poet, who talks
about us in obscure verses nobody
reads for sure, Lucia,
who laments that someone in the family,
her twin, committed suicide, but it can't be
true, she has no twin, I'm the second born
and a full year younger than she is.
Lucia is *putane* because she doesn't live
at home and because she won't say hello
or pretend to like uncle Joe
whom she calls a macho pig.
Secretly I know she has nothing
to say even though she pretends
to write and the family is ashamed
of that gypsy daughter, that bohemian, that cuckoo's
egg in our nest.
Sometimes we wish she were dead.
Sometimes we wish she were married.

At every family gathering
I pull out the accordion.
I play like a full orchestra,
overtures from Verdi and Rossini,
the music he loves,
the music I've learned by heart
as an act of love.

Out of the musical box spring
the burnished grapes in wicker baskets
of Italia, the Apennini breathe with lungs
that are the bellows of my accordion,
La Maiella scratches his snowy cap
among the Abruzzi mountains, the grand
old man, I've never seen but I've watched
my father's head grow white then bald.
The roads,
the mountain roads,
winding up
the steep flanks,
the round shoulders of the hills,
the geography of hearts,
winding up like a convoluted thought about someone you love,
how you can never understand them
how loving them is an act of faith,
a way of choosing to live
or to die by instinct,
something that you just can't back out of.
You can't really love unless you realize that a mortal life isn't
time enough to love anyone not
time enough to know yourself,
so I love my father, who is from the beginning,
who stood to make water
and lay down to make love to my mother,
who knew me from the beginning
as a vague stirring in his loins,
as a burst of ecstasy on a Sunday morning.

Lucia has other notions about love.
About love she says she's expert.
I don't know when she adopted the sacred heart
of eros. Five years after she left the church,
she was still a miracle worker of sorts.
I never could understand how she had the visions
while I had the faith,
except that she was the prodigal daughter

and I was the one who resented the fact
that she was not punished, but rewarded,
for doing whatever she wanted to do.

Lucia says that love is a labyrinth:
you approach a familiar doorway,
the door is wide open or barred shut,
the door is too small or too big for you
to reach the handle,
the door is the first hurdle,
then you enter the tunnel,
frescoes and graffiti blister on the walls,
the light you walk by never
fails to reveal a shadow,
you are searching for the one you think you
love through passageways that lead
nowhere but back into the self.
What I really think about love is all mixed up
in my head with what I remember being taught as a child
in religion class at school, the lessons I parrot today
to another generation of squirming innocents.
The family is the first experience
and then what the priest has to say
is a kind of generalization,
the holy family being a prototype
for relationships sanctified by the church
and sanctioned by the state. I remember how
impatient this model of divine grace
working in the world made Lucia.
She was an artist and therefore a narcissist
and believed, when she believed anything at all
that a person's relationship with God had more
to do with the way you love yourself.
Yet we would pray at the shrine of Mary,
light candles and for her they flared,
for me they smoked. I couldn't understand it.
We were ten and eleven years old,
and she would talk about the ancient rites,

the old gods and the new gods,
as if they were related and equal,
mythology and religion,
a pagan temple and a Catholic church.
Yet she would have her prayers answered,
(whatever she really wanted she seemed to get)
while my prayers, addressed to Jesus,
to God, the Father, in His name,
by which He was bound to answer,
were like conversations on a pay telephone,
He never rang back.

Every night I'm afraid I'll wake up
dead and find Lucia there before me,
that even my death will be a hand-me-down.
I know that I'm afraid of getting to the bottom
of the differences between us,
as if to really know her
would be to lose my soul,
and all the clothes she wore before me,
were gifts of shed skin
or cast off experience.
I made them my own and found
the fit gave me form.
I didn't give a fig about fashion,
but second hand clothes from my sister
identified me as hers.

Lucia wanted to be smarter
in her life than in her books
making me the butt
of her poems. She would experiment
with herself in that way,
putting me in the pigeon box of her words,
watching to see what would happen,
not prepared to make any mistakes
of her own. She demanded some
clarity of purpose in her life,

she wanted to act with a vengeance,
not because she was mad at anything
but to clear up the confusion,
a dusty room gave her a headache,
a Marx Brothers film would send her
running out of the room screaming.
In health class the film of a birth,
the untidy womb giving expression
to an anonymous morass of mucus and blood,
the human shape, a fish on a line,
made her sick and I heard her say:
'Never, never, never...'
in the darkened room,
and as the lights came on, I noticed she had
unbuttoned her shirt and was staring down
at her breasts. I think she feels
the same way about the family,
I think that by denying us she thinks
she can deny that she has legs,
that she's a woman, like any other woman,
servant to a dark blood she doesn't understand.

I'm not ambitious,
I find my art in the accordion
that entertains our uncles,
that makes my father hum
and my mother proud at weddings,
I always play and I don't mind,
in fact, I enjoy it,
but more when Lucia's not there
with her sulking face and rude
staccato laughter,
with that you're wasting yourself look,
half pity, more contempt.

But when a woman's life is so
worthless, I think she's got a perfect
right to do nothing,

to paint her nails,
to bake a cake,
and to wait for a man
to buy her shoes
so that she can go walking with him
on a Sunday afternoon
eating ice cream.
Not that I'm waiting for one,
but I like to be with friends
and to exchange tips on the latest
lipstick. I like it red, smear on the same
shade mother always wears.

Lucia and I would play when she wasn't looking
and paint big mouths with her rouge no. 5,
our lips quivering like blue gas flames
with excitement, as we prepared to look
like women. Mother says a woman's always
naked without her lipstick on.
One day I entered her bedroom alone
not prepared for the amazing transformation
I achieved by carefully drawing a cupid's
bow mouth with quick smooth strokes.
It stopped me for a moment as I looked up
from the lips I was defining
to see my skin, startling white,
my eyes, more intensely blue,
my hair, serenaded by the light
from the balcony,
and I saw that I was beautiful,
and I thought I must be rich,
and I thought there was nothing else
I needed to do. Then Lucia barged in,
grabbed the lipstick and painted her
nose bright red, ripped open her
blouse, her breasts, moulted birds,
and shouted that a woman always seems
naked without her lipstick on,

and her ironic laughter brought mother in
and a tanning for both of us.

Friday night when I'm going nowhere
and I'm alone, I play with my kohl
eye pencils and become Cleopatra.
Friday night and I know what it means to enter
a room with the sparkling white heart
of a refrigerator. I outline my eyes
like a cat so I can look at myself
in nine different ways,
Friday night and I watch the late show to learn
the Hollywood way to nirvana,
to a celluloid face and a polyethelene figure,
which tells me more about being female
than the poetry of Emily Dickinson
or the epistles of Saint Paul.

But I learn most about being a woman
from watching my mother, Alma.
I learn from her how a woman is made for love
and for cleaning house.
She's very fat from eating the insults of my father
who takes for granted her loyalty
and dreams divorce, dreams younger
women. He'll never leave her though
because the family's a landscape
he doesn't want changed.

For me she's the ring of smoke the wind wears
on the left hand, on the fourth finger,
open and generous, if somewhat gratuitous,
like a house built for birds,
a house with an entrance, but no door,
a house with a window, but no pane,
a house where the wind never begs
at the front steps for nothing.

I have to admit I'm happiest when Lucia's visiting
and we all work together as in the old days
preparing preserves of vegetables from the garden for
winter eating,
peeling the burnt skins back from roasted peppers,
pulling off the black ash that sticks
to the fingers in brittle chips,
pulling off the pepper tops,
watching the oil squirt then run
along our fingers, an orange sticky drool,
watching what I'm doing and doing it well.

I confess there was a time I wanted to be
like Lucia, when I thought her incredibly wise,
when I thought it courage that made her leave home
and generosity that made her experiment with love.
I remember how she used to say
with what seemed such a special kind of knowledge:
'I love you, no matter who you are,
that's not logical, but the axiom
on which logic depends.'
I guess it's something like the love we learned about in
church or from mother, it's so big and so perfect
it's like a circle drawn on a blackboard,
the imaginary lines of the imagined perfection
and then erased with an unthinking brush
by a monitor after class. But Lucia couldn't leave
home without coming back too,
whenever she claimed to be flat broke or in despair,
she couldn't stop being the centre of attention.

Disappointment is the unthinking brush
bloated with chalk dust and the promise of
a better life. I only want my fair share.
I want what's mine and what Lucia kicks over.
I want father to stop mooning about her and
listen to my rendition of 'Mimosa'.

So much of my life has been wasted feeling guilty
about disappointing my father and mother.
It makes me doubt myself.
It's impossible to live my life that way.
I know they've made their sacrifices,
they tell me so often enough,
how they gave up their lives,
and now they need to live their lives through me.
If I give it to them, it won't make them young again,
it'll only make me fail along with them,
fail to discover a different, if mutant, possibility,
succeed only in perpetuating a species of despair.

Most of the time I can't even talk to my father.
I talk to my mother and she tells him what she thinks
he can stand to hear.
She's always been the mediator of our quarrels.
He's always been the man and the judge.
And what I've come to understand about justice
in this world isn't pretty, how often it's just an excuse
to be mean or angry or to hoard property,
a justice that washes away the hands of the judge.

Nobody disputes the rights of pigeons to fly
on the blue crest of air across the territory
of a garden, nobody can dispute that repetition
is the structure of despair and our common lives
and that the disease takes a turn for the worse
when we stop talking to each other.
I've stopped looking for my father in other men.
I've stopped living as the blonde child he loved
too well. Now I'm looking for the man
with the hands of a musician,
with hands that can make wood sing,
with the bare, splintered hands of a carpenter.
I want no auto mechanics, their hands blind

with grease and the joints of a machine.
I want no engineers in my life,
no architects of cages.
I want to be with the welders of bridges
and the rivers whose needs inspired them.

I learned to be a woman in the arms of a man,
I didn't learn it from ads for lipstick or watching
myself in the mirror. I learned more about
love from watching my mother wait on my father
hand and foot than from scorching novels on the best sellers lists.
I didn't think I could be Anna Karenina or Camille,
I didn't think I could be Madame Bovary or Joan of Arc,
I didn't think that there was a myth I could wear
like a cloak of invisibility to disguise my lack of self knowledge.

The sky is wearing snow boots already.
I have to settle things with my father
before the year's dead.
It's about time we tried talking
person to person.

More than a tired man, my father is such a lonely,
disappointed man. He has learned from keeping
his mouth shut to say nothing,
but he still keeps thinking about
everything.

'If I had the language like you,' he says to me,
'I would write poems too about what I think.
You younger generation aren't interested in history.
if you want people to listen to you
you got to tell them something new,
you got to know about history to do that.
I'm a worker and I didn't go to school,
but I would have liked to be an educated man,
to think great thoughts, to write them,
and to have someone listen.

You younger generation don't care
about anything in the
past, about your parents,
the sacrifices they made for you,
you say: "What did you do that for?
We didn't ask you!"
right, is that right?
These are good poems you have Lucia,
but what you think about Italy!
"a country of dark men full of violence and laughter,
a country that drives its women to dumb despair."
That's not nice what you say,
you think it's very different here?
You got to tell the truth when you write,
like the bible. I'm your father, Lucia,
remember, I know you.'

The truth is not nice,
the truth is that his life is almost over
and we don't have a common language anymore.
He has lost a tooth in the middle of his upper plate,
the gap makes him seem boyish, almost vulnerable.
It also make me ashamed.
It's only when he's tired like this that he can
slip off his reserve, the Roman stoicism,
the lips buttoned up against pain
and words of love.

I have his face, his eyes, his hands,
his anxious desire to know everything,
to think, to write everything,
his anxious desire to be heard,
and we love each other and say nothing,
we love each other in that country
we couldn't live in.

FULL CIRCLE: THE FRIDA KAHLO POEMS

Whatever passes through my head,
whatever sits on my tongue
made solemn by a sad and lovely mouth,
whatever preaches and makes the air
quick with yellow pollen
like a jack in the pulpit,
whatever forgets its flesh and fashions itself
from the mineral body of the earth,
whatever fits together like a chain of hydrocarbons,
whatever empties itself of essential organs:
heart, liver, brain, uterus,
and makes of itself an abalone shell
for the greater song of the sea to sing in,
whatever the water gives me, I give back
with an open and singing mouth.

I   THE GIFT

That was the gift that was given me
when my legs were taken away,
awarded as a child from an attack of
polio that made my paint brush limp,
a defect I disguised in tin and canvas
and bright Mexican colours.

I swapped my girl's body
for a structure less sublime.
They gave me wheels for feet
and a square trunk
built with Lego blocks,
Lego woman with nerves
of fine copper wire
and a head that screws
on like a bottle cap.

There are no accidents.
I can't just spill paint on canvas
and call it . . .life . . .
the metal hand rail of the streetcar
that pinned me like a small white moth
to the floor of the collapsing bus
broke my foot, cracked the column
of my spine, smashed my pelvis,
and rendered me more fragile
than a reed boat in a torrent.

Dying didn't happen in a minute,
it took 29 years.

My crippled body became my fault.
Pain and that skeleton like a monkey
sitting on my shoulder,
a constant reminder of my natural
end. A September day plotting

to stop Frida cold:
you will not paint your masterpiece,
you will meet the man
Diego, who shapes the world
of wheels and running,
you'll love with all the sense
of a wooden doll
carved under the knife,
with brains of sawdust,
you will love
but you will waste your breath
trying to make another one like him,
one you can hold in your arms though he's
twice your size,
one you can be both big and little for.

III FEET OF CLAY

Hospital days and nights were colourless . . .
I learned to paint in bed on my back
and time wormed its way along like an old
river of red pigment,
precious and slow,
and hospital nights and days were colourless . . .

My feet were bruised spades
digging into the earth a grave for Frida,
my feet that were always in shadow
dragging the whole of me
underground,

but my heart was a thin tin plate
polished by too much wanting,
my heart was polished tin
that doubled the light,

the further my feet tunnelled
the more my hair climbed
like a trellis of morning glory
with its blue open eyes.

IV WHY I APPROACHED HIM

It wasn't humility,
it was a sense of female destiny
that drove me to show
my first sketches to Rivera
the greatest painter in the world.

It wasn't modesty
that made me flush
when his penetrating eye
scanned my pictures,

when that golden iris made its heady sweep
across the field of my dress.
My hopes were a flurry of wings
when a hawk's in the chicken yard.

It was my pregnant heart
with its secret load of vanity
and fear and desire,
a heart that descended
from its upper compartment,
neighbour to the lungs,
to pulsate in my pink silk pants.

V UNDER THE KNIFE

I paint the tears on my face
like small pickled onions.
My bed is all the landscape
has to offer and a knife,
the scalpel of Pittsburgh steel
wielded by a Detroit doctor.

My body oiled and tagged,
my blood clogged in poor plumbing,
not an orchid am I,
not even a shell that a snail could sleep in,

with so much blood I can't keep it
all on a single canvas,
it stains the frame,
it oozes onto the floor
of my studio.

In a basement room of an American hospital
next to an appendix in formaldehyde
my son floats in a jar.

VI I AM DIEGO

I have slept in these clothes before.
My heart no longer loves me
so Frida forgets who she is.
This suit is too big
and needs pressing

or I'm too little
like the carcass of a turkey
after the dinner
fit only for soup
or the garbage.

I am Diego.
I sit in his chair.
I sign Rivera.

Because my chair won't leave me
I can sit secure,
my legs apart,
my feet firmly planted
in shoes that are no bargain to fit.

I'm not going bald,
all the wine I drink
encourages my hair to stay rooted
or slip off my head like a skull cap.
I found female envy and waves
of long dark hair strewn on the floor
dank as seaweed.

Now I brandish the scissors
that cropped Frida's hair.
I am Diego,
the greatest painter in the world.

VII AND LAUGHTER HAS GOOD LEGS

Laughter's like the gurgling of spring
water from a hole in the earth
but sometimes it's like a breech birth
strangled in the womb.

When laughter has good legs
its cadence is an Olympic athlete
lighting with his torch
every corner of the room.

My laughter does not limp,
my laughter does not drag
its long skirt in the dirt,
it runs fingers through Diego's hair,

it unbuckles his pants,
it makes no bones about loving
the sun,
the smell of green

paint, the hair
like a dark sponge
under water,
the way the arched brows join

like the charcoal outline of a bird's flight
across Frida's face.

SO IT BEGINS

Whatever passes through my head,
whatever sits on my tongue
made solemn by a sad and lovely mouth,
whatever preaches and makes the air
quick with yellow pollen
like a jack in the pulpit,
whatever forgets its flesh and fashions itself
from the mineral body of the earth,
whatever fits together like a chain of hydrocarbons,
whatever empties itself of essential organs:
heart, liver, brain, uterus,
and makes of itself an abalone shell
for the greater song of the sea to sing in,
whatever the water gives me, I give back,
with an open and singing mouth.

LES PLAISIRS DE LA PORTE*

Women do not touch doors.

They know nothing of its pleasures: they can only observe
how it swings open miraculously as a man hurries forward
and administers a sharp rap and then, sometimes, almost for-
getting her, holds the door in his arms. She may rightly fear
encountering its rough wood swinging back against her nose;
she may, more rightly, put out her hand to ward it off.

If she catches sight of a brilliant world suddenly opening . . .
he will enter before her, and if he waits and makes way for
her, she knows how she must follow.

* a parody of a poem by Francis Ponge

PROOF THAT I DON'T EXIST
OR
THE LOVER'S DISCOURSE

He's not thinking about me as he
waters the dwarf palm by the window,
so green and alive in his life.
Yes, when he talks to plants they
blossom. I can see him cross
the room and trip
on the rug folded into a corner
so that the door won't stick.
One day he'll cut it to fit.
He's not thinking about me as the cat purrs
around his ankles for her supper,
the cat is golden and sleek,
the cat is an aristocrat and aloof
but low enough to beg for a meal,
I can't beg,
I would rather eat my tongue.
He's not thinking about me as he sniffs
his Napoleon brandy, I'm not French
nor a general, there's no trace of me
as he sips his five star cognac.
He doesn't need to know me to appreciate
that luxury. He's not thinking about me
as he changes his shirt, as he buttons
the little mother-of-pearl buttons of his best
shirt, the blue shirt with the canary stripes.
He's not thinking about me as he lights
another cigarette, when he draws
in the smoke, his body
relaxes without me, he burns
out his life in foul smelling ash.
He's not thinking about me when he looks
up at the night sky as he strolls
across Bloor Street to his favourite bar,
in long strides with his arms swinging.

31

The stars have his shallow wishes,
but deep enough for me to drown in.
He's not thinking about me
therefore I don't exist.

AS IN THE BEGINNING

A man has two hands and when one
gets caught on the belt and his fingers
are amputated, then patched,
he cannot work. His hands however
are insured so he gets some money
for the work they have done before.
If he loses a finger he gets a flat sum
of $250. for each digit &/or $100. for a joint
missing for the rest of his stay on earth,
like an empty stool at a beggar's banquet.
When the hands are my father's hands
it makes me cry although my pen keeps
writing, although my pen blots what's most
precious to me. Cannibalizes this crisis.
To you my father is a stranger and perhaps
you think the insurance paid is enough.

Give me my father's hands when they are not
broken and swollen,
give me my father's hands, young again,
and holding the hands of my mother,
give me my father's hands
brown and uncalloused, beautiful
hands that broke bread for us at table,
hands as smooth as marble
and naked as the morning,
give me his hands without a number
tattooed at the wrist, without the copper
sweat of clinging change,
give me my father's hands

as they were in the beginning,
whole,
open,
warm
and without fear.

NECESSARY SUGAR

I watch you sleeping by the window
where the horse-chestnut breathes,
its white candelabra blooms
aflame in the solemn mass
of the sun. Giving birth

I realized that men build cathedrals
in an attempt to sculpt light.
You are the firefly I collected
between my legs. A fiction

that last summer's romance had
to write, for your father, for myself,
not believing love could be a lie
even if mistaken. However the years

tell this story to you
already June has ground up
the petals strewn across the walk
like a welcoming carpet for a queen
under the wheels of my shopping-cart.

My little bag of sugar, ten pounds,
I carry you in the corduroy snuggli,
my kangaroo pouch
or the house a man might build
for his love to grow in.

POEM FOR MY DAUGHTER

Toys, the blue rhinoceros with the spidery
lashes, the monkey coyly seeing no evil,
hands velcro'd over his eyes, a truth
barrier, his long sad tail, the flower
rattle, the pink squeegie and a cloth
Indian doll whose black braid you use
to tug her along, these are the gifts you have
so far to know yourself.

Emily, these baubles that people your world
have no desires of their own, baby
woman, what can I tell you to try to
be without being

wrong? Try to live intelligently and
be happy as you are!
as your mother read too many books
thinking she could not be pretty.

A single season may strike campfires
in a man's blood. Keep what you feel
underground. Only the lead in your pencil
as you note these things
need poison your reflection
wanting the power that can make old
bones rise. Few men may come

back from the dead for you!
I know this because I have found
a man's duty a cold bed to sleep in
and his lust a fast train.

Because you are not unique,
you who have so soon discovered
your hands and feet,
and because even Sartre betrayed

the incomparable Simone
de Beauvoir for every half-
baked dish in Paris, I advise you to steel
yourself, although there's no escape
from pain, you may blaze bravely
and endure as iron in the fire.

BLOODY MARYS

You meet your husband at half-past ten
for drinks, leaving the daughter he donated
from his sperm bank with your mother,
he tells you about the woman who'll
sing in his bed tonight,
he tells you how her throat is adorned
with white camellias,
how she moves to his instrument
as a line of jazz,
totally improvised, always exciting,
and because you are never less
than a civilized woman, you ask her
name as you order another Bloody
Mary and shift uncomfortably
on furniture designed to be seen,
sitting out this dance around
the prickly pear, sex, the big
bang, then the whimper.

MANIFESTATIONS OF ICE

The voyage, a study in geriatrics,
no lovers on this cut-rate cruise
to Alaska, one week punctuated
by the dinner buzzer,
attempting shrimp cocktails,
those abortions huddled in red sauce.

Completely bald, the baby at three months
looks like your father.

I'm well cooked in my passion for words
in my belief in their efficacy.
If I say 'love' with the right emphasis
the glaciers will retreat
in the same way a new language
incubated in caves
caused the ice to back off
10,000 years ago
and our garden will produce
steak-house tomatoes,
herbs as fine as French
tarragon, bell peppers and for the birds
pumpkins gone to seed.
Not just a shit-box for every stray
cat in the neighbourhood.

*

Trees looming like bank towers,
glaciers trapping boulders
the size of tanker-trucks, soiled
ice, experienced of weather and earth,
hard-won jewellery of its flanks:
indigo, emerald and turquoise,
what I envisioned as clear
as the cubes chilling our drinks.

Alaska is huge and rugged and raw
and I step on shore with my European
dimensions. Here fireweed grows
to the stature of sunflowers while violets
remain the size of peas. Here Gulliver might
make one stop for two of his voyages.

Stepping into a grove of fireweed
our apparitions are captured in colour
by your camera for Sunday slides
shown between naps while the glacier
growing out of your Vancouver bedroom
inches its way into the livingroom.

If I say take me back to that summer,
you might imagine I remember it as happy,
even now I know better,
and that infant, emaciated on my bitter milk,
that waif who slept more soundly in a shoe
box at sea than in her home, that child
alone commands the thermostat
where I live, her small hands
exploring my face in the dark,
innocent tarantulas,
to bind and gag me in silk
so that my love need never
escape her attention,
my heart wanting her and wanting to fly
like a bird against glass.

All I have is this body, a bit of cloying fruit,
compact sweetness as found in dried figs,
to hold on to what we described as
tomorrow,
sailing into the midnight sun
who hesitates on the horizon like an old man,
too low to bother with suicide.

TRANSLATED WORLD

My daughter before she knows
she is human, might be content
to nest with birds, to lap water
from a bowl with the cat and to feel
in the likeness of her blush to peaches,
the fruit itself plumping her cheeks,

knows the language of other animals:
chimpanzees and their kennings,
parrot talk like poetic refrain,

knows our garden and its flowers
without their names of tulip, lilac,
or daffodil that I announce,

revels in the lawn, under the sky.
I ask what's blue, what's green?

GRAVITY*

You are trying to write a love scene
from a female point of view.
You want to write about sex
without writing a parody
of men's dectective fiction:
He was a long cool blond
precise as ice cubes.
His alibi was as contrived
as affection for a pet rock.
With the cautious deference
awarded a neighbour's dog
she patted his erection.
You were trying to write a love scene
in which love has nothing to do with it.

You would really prefer to write another scene
in which a woman makes love to a man
as if he were a woman,
but you can't write about sexual desire
without writing about penetration,
without writing about hunger, blind drive,
the exacting nature of sex.

You are overwhelmed by white water
when you wanted a lake,
contained and with the song of a loon
punctuating the stillness
like the several syllables
whispered in the dark
making up your husband's name.
Instead you get Niagara Falls,
Marilyn Monroe being murdered by Joseph Cotten,
electric power bills.

It's not easy to write a loving sex scene:
a man and a woman who are dear

to one another,
who will later have breakfast,
read the papers.
Where's the titillation in that?

They drive to Stanley Park
with their child between them,
belted into a booster seat.

They speed across Granville Bridge.
Below, as if in praise,
rise the riggings of sails.

A Sunday afternoon driving across water
where it feels as if they're flying above it all,
immune to gravity.

* 'Gravity' was written in response to Raymond Carver's poem,
'The Blue Stones'

LIFE IS THEATRE
OR
O TO BE ITALIAN IN TORONTO
DRINKING CAPPUCCINO ON BLOOR STREET
AT BERSANI & CARLEVALE'S

Back then you couldn't have imagined
yourself openly savouring a cappuccino,
you were too ashamed that your dinners
were in a language you couldn't share
with your friends: their pot roasts,
their turnips, their recipes for Kraft
dinners you glimpsed in TV commercials—
the mysteries of macaroni with marshmallows!
You needed an illustrated dictionary
to translate your meals, looking to the glossary

of vegetables, *melanzane* became eggplant,
African, with the dark sensuality of liver.
But for them even eggplants were exotic
or alien, their purple skins from outer space.

Through the glass oven door
you would watch it bubbling in pyrex,
layered with tomato sauce and cheese,
melanzane alla parmigiana,
the other-worldiness viewed as if
through a microscope
like photosynthesis in a leaf.

Educated in a largely Jewish highschool
you were Catholic. Among doctors' daughters,
the child of a truck driver for la Chiquita banana.
You became known as Miraculous Mary,
announced along with jokes about virgin mothers.

You were as popular as pork on Passover.

You discovered insomnia, migraine headaches,
menstruation, that betrayal of the female
self to the species. You discovered despair.
Only children and the middleaged are consolable.
You were afraid of that millionth part difference
in yourself which might just be character.
What you had was rare and seemed to weigh
you down as if it were composed of plutonium.
What you wanted was to be like everybody else.
What you wanted was to be liked.
You were in love with that Polish boy
with yellow hair everybody thought
looked like Paul Newman.
All the girls wanted to marry him.
There was not much hope for
a fat girl with good grades.

*

But tonight you are sitting in an Italian cafe
with a man you dated a few times and fondled
fondly until the romance went as flat as the froth
under the domed plastic lid of a cappuccino ordered
to-go. And because you, at least, are committed
to appearing mature as well as urbane
in public you shift easily into the never-
theless doubtful relationship of coffee to conversation.

He insists he remembers you as vividly
as Joan Crawford upstaging Garbo in *Grand Hotel*.
You're so melodramatic, he said, *Marriage
to you would be like living in an Italian opera!*

Being in love with someone who doesn't love you
is like being nominated for an Oscar and losing,
a truly great performance gone to waste.
Still you balanced your espresso expertly
throughout a heated speech without spilling a single
tear into the drink, after which you left him to pay the bill.
For you, Italians! he ran out shouting after you,
life is theatre!

FRENCH KISSES, BLUE BRASSIERES

Blue is lavander in the lamplight,
you imagine life simply
as a mutliple of seventeen,
the twilight traces a deeper texture
on your jeans, a thin tank top, new nipples
erect and brittle as candied violets.

From romance languages we learn
the moon has a female sex,
but *muguet des bois* too dark to see,

sweet, not sexy,
even given a French name,
language from which we borrow
words for intimate apparel,
secretive words, *lingerie, negligée, brassière,*
and *eau de toilette* of *muguet des bois,*
a scent girls choose for their first proms,
their hips filling out with crinolines
and ambiguous lusts
revelling in those swishing sounds
of *peau de soie* and *tulle.*

Overwhelming sweetness of perfume
from white and serrated lips
of the daintiest, most precocious of lilies,
with their common knowledge of dark wood,
drenching the senses,
a fragrance you can almost taste on your tongue,
bitter as a sip of *My Sin.*

You must close your eyes as you walk
steeped in an English melancholy memorized
from lines of Wordsworth or Keats. This way,
in the dark, you see clearly
as white chalk markings on a blackboard.
You remember a tree illuminated as if by an inner
light, not like Casa Loma flooded with spots,
enlarged and falsified as landscape in a postcard.

And lilies, around your ankles, hidden in the lawn,
as pretty, as delicate as Victorian undergarments,
composed in white lace and sheer muslin,
prissy, and their scent, cloying.
They merely flirt with the senses.

MOON SHARKS

Dark is deluge.
We grope for a way back from the river,
we grope for words to celebrate cosmologies
of wood, moss, fern, and quick
clean trout. Pre-Copernican, our language
says we have observed the sun
set. How little we understand
of one another, even here, close as twins
bobbing in the embryonic sac, night,
where only the larger heart is heard beating.

They say the dark is romantic
and the passionate are prone
to drowning, as if wading
through a Van Gogh canvas, *Starry
Night*, your sky bleeds in blue
black waves, and your stars are untouchable,
radiant jelly fish stinging the eyes.

Through the woods you can watch air thicken
as if absence of light makes molecules huddle,
liquefy. The languid motion of our limbs as if
walking through water, as if
we had lost our way and floundered
back into the river.

We strain to see and our vision
has the grainy texture of video.
Night was made for listening.
Because sound undulates
the ear is shaped like a conch.

An ear, dismembered is a strange gift,
the same basic structure as a shark:
cartilage and flesh, full of biographies,
mangled parts.

We follow slowly and we need time.
I grasp for this man's hand
out of what need? Like a flashlight
in the dark? In white slacks he walks
with the legs of the moon!

Having lived all night with gills
we go back to our beds, a peculiar breed.
Soon a sun will rise like yesterday's
and the atmosphere adopt its usual gaseous
state, only the grass somewhat wet from a night

underwater.

SNAPSHOT

*I work from awkwardness. By that I mean I don't like to arrange
things. If I stand in front of something, instead of arranging it, I
arrange myself.*

Diane Arbus

If Diane Arbus hadn't been born a woman
she would have had an operation

because a woman understands the body best
as surrender to spectacle:
the super beautiful, the bearded lady,
the tycoon, the tattooed man
stretching his skin for canvas,

because nothing came between her
and her cameras,
because she wore them like jeans
shrunk to fit in a bathtub

(it makes walking difficult)

because she was swamped in equipment,
clumsy as a child playing dress-up,
because she waited, balanced in ballet shoes,
for the right moment,

that was her skill,

because she wintered in black leather skirts,
because she tried to make love
survive sex orgies,

because she is forgotten as a photographer
of children, because she worked in fashion,
because negative space plays hard to get,

you thought she was just snapping
freaks—
she caught what you wouldn't see:
your averted eyes, your face behind
the box— because knowing how to frame
anything alive makes it art,

because she felt lost but couldn't
remember how it happened.
Setting the Leica on self-timer
then rushing into her subject's clothes.

FALSE ANALOGIES II

I know at least one book
arguing men and women
evolved from different species.
Women cry more easily because
they still carry so much of the sea

in their bodies. It makes them feel in-
complete, lonely for a self that gets

harder and harder
to define. Tears, blood, and amniotic fluid
have the same composition as seawater.

Religion comes more easily to women
because a regular release of hormones
makes their bodies swell as if with tides.
In pregnancy they carry fifty percent more
fluids in their bloodstream. So the feeling
some theologians describe as 'oceanic'
comes naturally to them.

Only that dark bosc pear, the uterus
can conract and retract; more than male
muscle, a dwarf star.

Men, those extraterrestrials, angels
or devils made a truck stop here
for mother and home cooking.

ROME WASTED IN THE RAIN
for Antonio D'Alfonso

I find my way through this city
like a woman through the arms
of a married lover. To test
myself as I am, clinging
yet tentative, I need to
know his loyalty lies

elsewhere. I want that bush
I cannot name walking without
a field guide in a city
sucked of sunlight like raw
egg through a minute fissure
in an otherwise perfect shell.

In the rain, the smell of things is amplified
as a cacophony of pharmaceuticals, of
rare perfumes, incense and exhaust
mixing in the maze of streets. My red
leather shoes step into some, what I pray,
is no more than dog shit. In Rome it reeks of regret
that bed of nails reserved for the guilty,
only a yogi, no young mother
who's left her child to come here
rests on comfortably.

Junkies sit on the Spanish steps
where the azaleas are overwhelmingly
magenta, there I strain for ions of
Keats electric in the atmosphere of bells
rising from a thousand churches.

Trees by the Tiber and in each oasis
trunks studded with hypodermics —
heroin, that derivative of opium.
The romantics continue to indulge
in hallucinations and self-absorption.
An Alpha Romeo backs into a chariot,
time is that compressed when
you're drugged or in love.

A blue umbrella pokes out where
a woman makes her bed in a door-
way. A makeshift roof,
a bit like the blue of heaven
on the avenue to the Vatican.

Nothing is resolved except
in the intense firing of
porcelain or passion
where I find even the mistakes
too good to throw away.

THE PRIMER

With the smell of hyacinth across the garden
Recalling things that other people have desired.
                                    T.S. Eliot

1

No, she doesn't remember what was
spoken in another language.

2

Yes, she does remember smaller
matters, some dimes, bright but
misting in the palm. She remembers
sticks of Doublemint gum, their dusting
of sugar, she remembers unwrapping the odour
of synthetic mint, she doesn't remember
chewing but if the package was nearly empty
the man would let her keep the whole
thing. With the scented cyclinder
she could whistle for the darkness
at the end of light-
ed tunnels. What was her body
but a magician's box with a false bottom
for disappearing
into and allowing
herself
        to be
sawed in half?

3

        Without wounding there's *no* art!
O *no*, such a brilliance
defied her, it deified her.

49

4

The gum is mnemonic.
To bring back the experience
I buy some now for her, slide
out all six sticks
as if there were a choice
to be made. She picks
one and puts it aside.
If this is our journey to the
underworld she must eat
nothing or
            not return.

The sugar powder takes the imprint
of her fingers, a confectioner's
sugar so fine it's like flour.
One finger touches her lips
as if to savour

as if for silence
the gesture in alternating currents
of strength and fragility.
O irritating iridescence,
O white moth immolated by moonlight.

5

Within the foil tube
an expanding tableau,
ECCO the universe before it was
a small white room
with a single bed and sunlight
on the sheets,
the hot white gift
of detergent and bleach.
The girl is rumpled,

O the girl is layered
as an onion and tearful and tight.
                              The girl is six

years old behind a locked
door. He pulls her panties down.
Because of something he can't feel
he touches.   *Yes*

what he calls absolution
she knows as incontinence
and it shames
her. She feels *nothing*
else. *Not* pain
though her blood burns
when his nail catches like a burr
her inner self abandoned
                              in a hurry

to exit from her *not* yet fledgling
sex, that bird in the nest
orphaned by his hand.

6

That she could say *yes*
or *no* was not yet understood. That's
understood. That she learned
to say *no* before she learned to say
yes may be significant. That with her *no*
he offered her greater gifts is *not*
surprising but knowledge
she has yet to put to good
use. That the greatest gift offered
was the gift of an English dictionary
may sound made up when I tell
you she grew up to write poetry.

That she rejected this gift
may account for her difficulty
in getting started and her equivocation
about the composition of this poem.

7

They think we're the same
but we're *not*, the writer
and the text. You see
she called me in to interpret.
They're immigrants and that's *not*
the whole story as you may suspect.
If I could tell it to you!
No, it's just what she remembers
perhaps just what she *wants*
to remember

                  that's all I've got to work with.
But what she forgets is just as important.
What she forgets is more
important.

8

She has *no* words in any language
that point, without her having to describe
what happened.

He held out the dictionary,
he did*n't* speak himself.

9

How can this be true?
You have*n't* heard his
voice. Just mine and an ink-
ling of what hers might be.

Is he mute? Is he tongue-
tied? Is commissioning me to write
this poem *her* way of getting even?

Is this poem surgical bandage
taped across his mouth?
                              or the bond

the hands make when they clasp

10

in anxiety
         in prayer

when they close

as if
         to cherish?

as if
         to grasp?

MUSIC, LITERALLY
OR
MAKE YOUR LIFE AN EAR !

Listening to Puccini is like having great sex with someone you
love. No, that can't be right. Listening to Puccini is both physical
and more so. The memory of great sex with someone you loved.
    When the sounds you hear are metasexual, it's Giacomo.
Though he has died,that ladies' man is not dead.
    Listening to Puccini is like being programmed with a laugh
track. You respond even when you don't know how to respond.
    Listening to Puccini is like being masterminded by the machi-
nations of a deranged Pavlovian psychologist. He keeps ringing
the bell. He forgets to feed the dog.
    That is what is meant by *hunger of the imagination.*

LA COULEUR DE LA CHALEUR

Red's for immediacy, for intimacy, for sensation,
Red's for courage, for cowardice, and for everything
not in between.
Red's for light when it dazzles
for light when it doesn't shine.
There's no stopping
what it stops.

Red's for love when you don't know how
to praise it or
to damn it.
Red means business, sex
when it's commerce, sex
when it's not.
red's for the escape
of affairs, of exits.

Red's for life, when it's hidden
death when it's spilt.
Red riots in tulip, in geranium, in ribbon.
Red likes ants in the pink
peonies. Red's ahhhhhhhhhhhhhhhhhhhh!
almost relaxing when it's rose
deadly when it's crimson!
Red's in the masticator
and in the
masti
cator
y.

Never camouflage, never reticence.
red just can't be red enough.

THE AFTERLIFE OF SHOES
for Gary Geddes

You, woman, have been dead long enough! Move
over. We gravediggers on Monday morning harry
the poor, the unidentified, buried in the heart
of the Santiago cemetery. The heart a black hole
wanting to suck everything up. Get up! Get out!
Even if you think you're tired. No loitering
for such as you, all skin and bones. Less
than what the cat drags in as a trophy.
The cat who cultivates a master of the plush
slippers. You there, Mizz So and So. Yes, you. Come here!
We have prepared a bath of pitch for you who unwound
in bubbles. Got yourself into trouble, did you? Let some macho
give it to you good. With his gun loaded.
Hey, take off that wedding band. It didn't stop you before,
screwing around. What's it made of? Gold? We'll keep it.
Copper? What your brother from the mines of Rancagua
            unearthed
let him take back. What do you say to that?

Take off your shoes. Take off your feet.
Hey, at last you're finished with working.
Finished with walking. What's wrong with that?
Now you can ride in chariots like the rich.
What are you waiting for? Still the revolution?
The revolution has died with you! No!
Leave behind that shoe with the platform heel.
It won't burn well and besides it is no longer in fashion.
It betrays you as one who died in the fall of '73.
Do you want them to kill you again? Stupid! Enough of this
heroism. It, too, is old hat. I'm like you but I can't stomach
worms, let me tell you, once is all I want to die.
I work for whoever pays me. Not you. Although there is no
politics for the dead, there's still the police
who have prohibited that foreigner from taking photos.
But this man is cagey for while the official

55

pedals ahead on his bicycle to beat him to the next stop
at the graves of the famous, he slips his camera out for a nobody,
and steals a portrait
of your shoe.* Overturned. Down at heel. Spilling

earth. He must have a fetish, this guy.
Heh, what's that you say? Speak up girl!
He almost arouses you. Why? Because with his dark beard
he reminds you of your husband? But what a pity!
All that's left of your figure is a small bone
in the refuse, a finger still wearing its cheap ring.
And it would take an Olympic gymnast to balance
all their weight on such a sliver.
You can't get up so you call
out while your remains boil in pitch. The smell
is like what the rain does to a barbecue.

Remember my breasts, Paco! Remember my lips!

I hear your voice like dry leaves underfoot
crushed. But what does the foreigner hear?
The beetles swarm to form a brassière. And that gringo
snaps another picture while the official
turns a blind eye. Thanks to goodwill
towards a visitor to his country. No bribe.

In this poem, the dead speak and the official is tolerant.
Which of these miracles will you believe?

*Ah, but the shoe is your lucky ticket! What's nascent in the roll of film,
in its image of your sole, finds immortality and your foot, and then the
Achilles and then the shin and so on . . . . The way the body is united.
The way Chile is not. Girl, he doesn't know it, but now, because of him,
you're a refugee in Canada, where from a simple foot, where, some say,
from a hangnail, they can clone an entire person.

INVITATION TO DARKNESS

What disturbs her most about that night are the dogs
snarling at scraps. The streets as if evacuated.
Worse than in New York, lost in Harlem where fires
raged in the middle of the roads. An invitation to darkness.
In the Santiago lamplight what she sees are canine ears
about to ignite the air with their listening.
The drone of the embassy car makes the hounds pause,
their dark noses sniffing perfume in the decay. She picks
her way to the back entrance to a row of white houses.
She lifts her skirt to avoid the filth. Through the filter
of blue light, her calves, milk-fed and vulnerable, gleam.
She imagines dogs lust for such legs. Pink as veal.

The moon is full. Its face made strange by the southern sky.
And she is walking upside
down from the lover left behind in Toronto.
What does that say about love? She can't imagine it
right side up again.

These Chileans move her strangely, as if she were
one of them. What is stranger than unrecognized
familiarity? Like the moon with that dark mask
we all disguise, the face we would wear
if our right half matched our left.
Her host confides that Chileans are twisted,
she wonders who is straight? Not her Canadian husband
who made her push him from her heart. Afraid of the woman
in himself.

At the dinner party to welcome her, a foreign writer,
she meets the wife of the man who has been pursuing the poet,
taking her picture over and over again with his camera.
His wife is a painter. Her nudes hang on the walls
of the house. The flesh of their torsos
is blue. The two women click.
The painter pulls the earrings from her ears and gives

them to the poet. It works better than voodoo.
They understand one another.

The painter is small and nervous. Her intensity strains
as if it were the Doberman, bigger than herself,
she walks in the park, with the leash
winding around and around her hand.
The struggle to control the animal makes her sad.
She can never enjoy her walk or a view
of the moon except as that luminous force that makes her pet
howl, his long tongue lilac in the moonlight.

What is it about the moon? That night in bed she fathoms
for the first time its power and refuses to lie
perfectly still but thrusts with her pelvis as her husband
mounts her, balancing himself on his elbows. Her legs plié.
Neither is the man immune to the moon. Making love
he presses on her knees for leverage and
floats to the ceiling, leaving her below,
those female thighs diminishing to wrinkles
in the sheets. From the window by the wing of a jet
the Andes look like that. In winter.
Everywhere the husband turns he feels fenced
in by his wife's legs. She is jealous of any
life outside her. No wonder he takes
the most precipitous route out of the marriage. Through the
skylight. No wonder he buys a ticket for Paris.
His plane climbs higher and higher. And the earth does not look
round to the free man.
                    The planet looks like some kind of platter
staggering in the hands of a drunken waiter
                                        about to spill
what the customer ordered,
                        to waste
what is meant to nourish.

SANS MERCI
for Gwendolyn MacEwen

If the song never dies. The problem is not silence
in the bones, but their piercing lyrics,
as if an Egyptian, sun-scorched sceptre
beat time. Within the marrow. Such rhythm.
That last fierce summer devoured.
You know the intensity of August
heat remembered, the pitch of cicadas,
their ecstasy or dying, rising
predictably as, by night, do the mercury
points of fever.

              The human face, hideous
in the dark is transfigured
by striking a match. Moving
through the unlit house, the end
of his cigarette is all you can see,
the red eye of the Cyclops.
When he disturbs your dreaming
the sheets catch fire.

              But you are cold.
Why does the volume of song
increase against the quiet
tick of household things?
The unwashed dish gathers the drip,
drip, like your two finger typing.
Incremental repetition. Tap, tap,
tap, the girl pecks at the keys
while the woman she has become is deep
in sleep. Her words are at ease when written
and distant and eternal as bird
tracks a scripture of stars in snow. Winter
solstice. The hemisphere hurtling toward
tonight. Their taste is tartar,
furs the gums, is aluminum on the tongue,

smacks of the residue from coffee
brewed in cheap percolators, such words
know miracles. Water turning to red
wine in rusty pipes.

It's not Despair, but her sister, Prophecy,
who, to finish you, conjures the dark god,
brings him panting to your bed like an old dog
with few tricks, and that jackal, Anubis,
out of curiosity or malice or something else,
cranks the dial inside your head until your ear
drums implode from the pressure of too much music,
the pressure of too much palpitating music in the mind.

DOVETAIL, THE VERB,
OR
HOW WE IN THE WORLD ARE ALL CONNECTED

A bird's wings,
at the point they fan
out,

when it's impossible
to tell
whether for settling

or flight

WITHOUT WILLING

The bare feet of Raphael's Christ ascending into a heaven
topped by the golden dome of St Peter's.
Jesus is buoyed by the light, by pigments
in white and blue. And by the luminous
air beneath his toes
unfolding like an inverted
                              parachute.

The clouds part to let
                          earthlight escape
while in the cathedral a gilded
skeleton holds onto the hour
                              glass about to run

out with this dusty equation,
this worship, not of the spirit,
                          but of the decay
of flesh, of the yellow
                  syphilitic Christ of Gauguin.

Eternal life's a hawk in the hand
                              of the taxidermist.
And wings still want something,
                              can you believe?
of air as they are perpetually
                          spread,
ready to glide over the divan,
even though the eagle's eyes glint
without willing as a water glass
achieves emptiness
                  and silence—

the musical notation
perfected in its
                  breaking!

LUMINOUS EMERGENCY

✻

How is it that we love
                    for the sake of what we loved
when what we loved
                    we would not go back to loving?

I

They say that landscape and language,
the ampersand, are imprinted in our minds
in the same way geese
fix on the first moving sign as Mother,
the way some love takes root
like crabgrass in the strawberries,
much deeper, much hardier
than the plant that fruits.

I remember Italia of the *praetutti*,
of Ovid, of D'Annunzio, of Silone,
of Hemingway's soldier boy self
in *A Farewell to Arms.*

                    And what I knew from the start.
Original.

II

From the back of my grandmother's house,
from her garden of pomegranate,
sunflower and grape,
I can see it all and rising to a greater height,
the snow-capped mountain, La Maiella, white sow,
brilliant as the naked shoulder of a god in moonlight,
brilliant as the cascading light at the back
as he ceremoniously turns revealing
wings. All da Vinci designed.

But what is moonlight to him?
or to us for that matter,
after even the briefest
pause by the Sea of Tranquillity?

III

We've been told that the angel doesn't distinguish
the living from the dead,
or earthlight from moonlight.
The angel doesn't need
the sun like a coal miner's cap
to tunnel through the darkness
to reach us, because angelic
light is always within,
as lightning-bug or firefly
hold their blazing inside
or we could call it outside if
for the angel there were a difference
but such presence drifts
through our atmosphere as if composed
of only a slightly heavier element,
the way, above the churning and dashing
of dark waves against rocks,
a fine spray flings itself across the sea

no longer one with water
yet also alien to air.

IV

This view from the hills opens
the landscape like surgery.

In my fingers the grapes are rubbed
    to glowing, the light
in their skins, as from dark rooms

or the candle's flame
ripening with midnight.

Such is memory
it darkens what it seems
to illuminate in time
whatever is preserved
    must also alter.

Like love loving us not.
                                For what we are.
For what we hide.

V

& the bell that used to stand to the side
of the church I played
in its inverted cup
                    doppelganger
for the clapper!

Then my left-handed music was unsung
before they changed me
                            with a pencil
before they changed me
                            with a stick.

&the bell that used to stand to the side
is enclosed in a new tower.
When the Angelus rings out birds
scatter:
            uccelli

                    uccellini...

my own daughter's first words,
Italian bird already having something
of the sky, *cielo,* in it

& singing sweetly singing as if
to me and I find myself happy
if this is true

            or not.

VI

In the field *farfalla*
as even in some living poet's journal
going from flower to flower,
not for clover but for red poppy,
their wings silk-screened and colour
their music of interval.

The bee is a golden earring,
a stinger in the jewellery,
it's *la vespa* for a country
no longer mine,
                but the stranger's
in me.

VII

For fauna in the mountains find
she-wolf, bear, and angel
to be seen as the wind's seen
making the trees more visible.

& if the planet were a bald husk
shucked like corn & all its green
silk consumed by lightning and moth,
logged and strip-mined to the nth
degree and if the planet were left naked or nuked,
how would wind or angel know themselves,
how would they know themselves without us
to scribble or turn up our faces
                        in reverence?

How would wind or angel deliver
their speaking in silence?

VIII

Before the operation, just to hear themselves
quack as a child, *paperino,*

paperino,
who would refuse anaesthetic
as the neurologist probes one part
then another of the brain?
Then it's one day then another
and you are speaking in tongues
as your life rewinds to a whirring
snap
        when faces surge to the surface

brilliantly lit as if by darkness
from which the figure in Rembrandt
emerges.
        Luminous.

IX

Look how I'm with her on the bench in the Villa delle Rose
by the fountain and the amputee
Greek and Roman statues.

Nonna hasn't lost weight,
                her soul
must also be
        consoled by carbohydrate,

while in the *mean* time like balloons
my lungs hold twice the oxygen
although my heart is still only this

                (big)

heart of hare, heart of hen,
heart of human smaller
than what remembers

                    (me)

X

That my tongue has been un-
Mothered. That my tongue has thickened
with English consonants and diphthongs,
mustard and horseradish. That burning.
That burdened.

While on my lips Italian feels
more free, like wind in the trees
when the window's sealed shut
and you're trapped inside a solitary
game of Scrabble.

No—English is not so cosy!
It's hypothermic. It's haunted
by ghost letters & gnomic,

                        for it is true

                *

that we love
                to forget we forget
to love.

ANGEL OF SLAPSTICK
for Bronwen Wallace

Light from the dust
of a drawer.

The beetles don't fly out when Dewdney opens his desk. No,
they show off their brilliance without stirring. The shining is
concentrated in their shells as if from a trace of what originally
moved them. Their legs have lost all urgency. Curled and
withered, they are blacker than in life. As if the light has drained
entirely into their armoured back. The backs are green. They are
glinting. All gold is fool's gold. What is most precious are these
once-living emeralds, which have inched their way, which have
known light as if it were a form of intention. The construction of
their wings splits the crystal of the back.

When short people sit down to drink tea, their feet tread air.
They exercise their ankles because their soles feel vulnerable.

'Evolution is on your side,' Dewdney reassured me.

(But not the design
of the furniture.)

Descended perhaps from something that crawled out of the skin
of one of the smaller meat-eating dinosaurs, from a relative of
tyrannosaurs, its crazy locomotion between flying and walking.

We have forgotten more than we know
about earth.

Flying with you to the West Coast
I tried to explain how my balance
was a special gift, an adaptation,
the smaller body a truce
between the oversized head and the planet.

It's fall 1981 and we are seated in the Air
Canada jet by the wing. Because you are ten
inches taller you can more easily command,
from the stewardess, drinks. You are ten inches
taller yet we have the same size feet.
'A deformity,' you say. And it's good to be
with you, Bron. That your walk is a form of ballet.
That your height is stature which cannot be measured.

All the things you have taught me and our place in the story I
can't get into one poem I can't mend even the simplest break with
this improvised sling

                              over the abyss.
When I recall your face.
Slowly. So that my life with you is replayed.
And I watch it like film. In the dark
my eyes fill, images dissolve,
bodies spill into one another and
become one body,
when it's erotic and not a mass
grave.

Rumi wrote that we are all like unmarked
boxes shifting from one thing
into another. Maybe we are like frames
in a film we can't just look
at the negatives.
The print. We have to run
the whole thing. Live
faster than we can be stilled.

Where else would I find how to make soup
and how to make poems on the same page?
At home with you, it is written
in the same language. So when a raisin from a curry
floats up in my fish chowder I think of you
the poet who understood *metaphor*

is still the Greek word for *porter*
and as Berger reminds us, the service better
rendered is not comparison, but transportation.
Our baggage. Our ghosts.
Not for simile, but for discovery

'of those correspondences of which the sum would be proof
of the indivisible totality of existence.'

Listen. What we can become together
without even thinking about it.
In spite of its small betrayals,
trusting the body.

Because I was thinking
of you, the way your magic
is in the domestic,
no tricks, just practical technique,
as simple as cracking eggs in half
with the slightest flick
of the wrists so that no little bits
of shell spoil the easyover or scrambled,
and at the same time I was looking up
for street signs, myopically
making my way out of *Badlands*
I had been reading in the subway
and I know I should have been
more fully there
for breathing until breath is
wind turned outside in
blowing through us cleanly
as those few ashes
spilling out of Carolyn's
purse. It's you. That ash not you.
You are Orpheus
scattered among your friends. Many.
You are many. Now even with the best

acoustics in the world, without wood,
without the body
of the violin,
where is music?
The bow saws to the applause

of one hand. Harmonious instrument.
When all we who miss you want is what was
heard off-key. The woman.

So because I was more with you than on Bloor
sidewalks, I was surprised when I looked down
and my feet were drawn into quicksand
from the Badlands. Even a little
reading can be a dangerous thing.

What really happened is that I had walked several feet without

sinking
into cement. Jumping out of my shoes as if my ankles knew
wings. And the man in the white
hat from Public Works said: 'How in hell
did you do that, lady!'
And you can have faith in this
Bron, in *public works* and the *common courtesies* .
IIe helped me. He found a pole to pull out my shoes,
cleaned them off and drove me to the library.
And I was on time.

So I think of my way of bumbling along on earth like those bees
which circumvent gravity and all we know of the laws of
areodynamics to fly, I think of that little feat, as a story I want
you to interpret. Stretching, by the ligaments of language,

not flight, the miracle is
not our altitude on the DC-7,
nor the birds we take for granted,
the birds in which we glimpse

from their fierce appetites, our familiars.
The first dinosaurs moving among us.

No, the miracle is not
in flight, but
in the bones of what may be
in time
whether winged or grounded,
whether ostrich or woman.

I might have continued
to look for redemption
by cement, for baptism
in gravel, sand and water,
if not for you. And the angel
of slapstick. And look
my feet take me without my head.
How far.
                    How near.

*'this gentleness we learn
 from what we can't heal.'*

                    Bronwen Wallace

SELF-PORTRAIT 1994

Symmetry in the moth is to attract a mate.

Asymmetry in art is not
                natural design,
not reproduction.
What's interesting if not beautiful's
                mismatched, unmarried.

Regard the face, the right brow is
                perfectly smooth,
while the left unfurls like a fan
                no, with something of the
masculine, the cock's comb,
                its ragged red end.

Ambiguity in shades of blue or green
                whether sea or weed,
the eyes in the mirror look
                to the silver backing.

The lips are parted as if
                to speak silence. The right
side is scarred, an accident, a bad
stitch job. The jaw
is squared, the cheekbones
                in love with line.

The generous nose is fleshy, full,
                born to gorge
on fragrance, hothouse odour of rose
pales before the kitchen smells of rice, risotto,
of basil, olive oil and garlic.

Now the face hides in the hands
                which belong to the father.

Now the mouth opens to sing

        an aria from *La Traviata*.

She is less mother

        than sibling or child.
She is less teacher

        than student or novitiate.
She is less writer

        than finger tracing
what it means to see

        blue in braille.

The poet turns away from the page, the pulsing

        cursor,
the WordPerfect and opens the door
for the reader

        who is her true lover.

'I've missed you, I've missed you so . . .'

FRAGMENT OF BLUE
for Patrick Lane

Because it is dark because
the room must be illuminated
and because in winter chill the crickets
retire their legs, those cellos locked in cases,
we write music as if we were caged,
as if we were the moths, white and thin-
winged stumbling against the pane.
Pressed against glass they become
living frost flowers. You lock out
their eggs laid in furniture, in wool,
in silence. Freezing rain and the violin's
song is cat
gut, not platinum wire, but the sound

74

the words, wisteria on the vine,
make in your mouth. Leonard Cohen
is still our man in stereo.
His voice crackles, black carbon,
from the fire, what is left
of wood, what is left of
Joan glowing in embers. You show
me a fragment of blue
tile from the baths of Caracalla.
You cannot lose Rome in this loose
mosaic of memory. You let me touch
the pure cipher, the ceramic bit.
Because I come from east of the Eternal
city, I know less than nothing.
I know silence and song
always in another language.
The poem stirs in the sternum
before it can be
scripted through the inky
darkness of Chianti. We will again
taste silence in these syllables
sipped from the body
of red wine, the body
a tongue both tender and tannic
for which I thank you, Patrick.

MY HART CRANE

'Language has built towers and bridges, but itself
is inevitably as fluid as always.'

I

There are no stars tonight save
memory, there are no stars.
Tonight the body disappears.
No stars—the constellation, Aries
is invisible, revised by the universe
of quasars and quarks. I stand on board a mere
marine vessel. Vision is a voyage. I feel
the rocking of waves, I feel
the deck bucking beneath my feet,
its worn wood. From near the end
of the century, I have travelled back
to get here, I have broken the space time
continuum someplace in the Caribbean where it's
midnight again in April, 1933, so I might

step into Hart's shadow. We see
no stars tonight, even the sea
is clouded over, murky. This is an elegy
for all of us, Harts, who want to change,
who make pacts with suicide and chance
it with the stars. We channel, is it neuroses,
into our leaping

                    into our fates? Murky. No moon,
no stars save memory. It's late, Dr K, the sky
is murky tonight. The sea is rocking.
Its lullaby has lured us from our berth
to a death somewhat cosier. There are no stars
the briny depths, a cistern of tears, a spittoon
full of sharks yet I'd follow you without a second

                                        thought through fathoms
I'd sink to stay put in the past

                              with you my beleagured
Hart. Whom have we abandoned
in the state room? Who expects us to come
back? The dark

cleft in the sky without
                              stars must be
remembered , the life
                                        lines un-

ravelled.

Because you could not love your own
body, your man
                    hood, your cover, your female
lover.
            Because I, because I

see no stars any night
                    save memory.

II 'RAPTURE / RUPTURE'

The sun is also a star making us
blind to all others like bridemaids
dimmed by the dazzlement of the
bride. That was me before Hart
started on the booze at breakfast.

Call me Peg Might-Have-Been-Hart-
Crane who travelled to Mexico for a quicky,
if not easy, divorce, but was waylaid
by love. I knew him already, he was
a friend of my husband's. But I never
knew the man who hit me. Yes, I said

Hart, you're a volcano! But I didn't expect
you to blow up in my face! How he could

singe me with a single word, though I never
minded because of the poetry, because
of his knack for making the language
sing! The art made it all right and that he
was so oddly sensitive writing verse
while playing music full blast,
but as for the town's church bells,
their clanging drove him crazy, he said,
sound's just noise when it's not composed,
he said, compared with that holy racket ,
our ship's propellers played Pachelbel.

It was lunch time. I had a headache and Hart
showed up in my stateroom unshaven and still
in his pyjamas to apologize the way men like to
do to blame the woman. He lamented my
clumsiness. But I had the sympathy
of the doctor and I had had it up to here with his heart-
felt apologies. Clearly that morning his guilt sparked
his greed for he ate all my congealing breakfast.
He managed to hide his despair in the pocket
of his robe, the crumpled telegram with an invitation
to live without me in Chagrin
Falls, Ohio. Happily, though his mother was dead ,
his father's wife was more welcoming.

Bankers and brokers are believed
to jump for less
or is it more? I get mixed up easily
but I do know that when the right side is
wrong you're driving
                              in a foreign country.

Like what Hart made of my boyish figure
attached to his mother's face. He was no
lover of falsetto but his grandmother was the

only woman he truly cherished. Her will,
a trunk full of love letters left him with a poet's
legacy, while his mother's divorce left him a

bankrupt. Bankers and brokers,
like those who have jumped
for less
         or was it more?

III 'A BOY'S LOVE FOR HIS MOTHER'
That hate is but the vengeance of a long caress.

Even if she had been the real Gioconda
she deserved that moustache. My mother,
how I remember her, Grace
Hart Crane. Without the Grace
she was myself. Without the Grace
she was the unguent, she was the grease
my sailor would smear on his self
before he rammed it into her baby,

Hart. It was never Peg I loved nor
mother nor the sea I sang in wornout tropes.
The sea's simply salt but sweat is also sweet.
No, it was another kind of drowning I preferred
down in the boiler room or onshore where
the jungle presses with hot love.

Sure the deck broiled with such impossible heat
that day my feet baked in their sneakers
like sole poached in parchment. That She
also burned at night was my fault I suppose
her hand might have been put to better
use, but she had to light that damn cigarette
herself . Bang! Bang! the Cuban

cigars exploded, a careless
accident and not my concern except
for the clumsy fact that someone so

small could stumble so
stupidly was all I thought there was to be
said about that unpleasant surprise.
But we fell, together, in love in Mexico
where She was divorcing another
man for less. Not that I
was drunk, not that I
had never been engaged before
more happily to the bottle
than to another woman. She didn't want

to forgive me. She idly watched her hungry man
eat her breakfast scraps, unshaven and in pyjamas!
and She didn't care that something was wrong
with *him*. She complained about a 'headache'.
How unfair when all the clamouring bells in Mixcoac
couldn't raise the slightest wrinkle of discomfort
on her brow. But for my sharp word , that pea, what a

pity, She became such a princess! Why
did I do it, you still ask, now that you know
Her story and are no longer on my side?
Dear reader, this is what upset me,
for the first time her distress seemed bigger
than mine and She had a witness, the doctor
who ordered me to go to hell! I didn't jump
to punish Peg, I didn't jump
to drown. The sea was so flat, so still,
its surface was pure mirror. I saw birds,
not fish, in the water, I saw wisps of fair-weather
cumulus drifting, not sargassum.
The sun below shone as brightly
as the sun above. It wasn't that I couldn't

swim but that I had never before aimed
so high. I didn't plunge to drown, I leapt

                                        to fly.

IV 'THE HOUR OF PAN'

It wasn't storm, it was calm.
It wasn't cold or midnight
as one might expect it was
hot and high noon. It was the hour

of Pan, of panic, when the shadow
has no where to go but back
into the self. And the water was not wine
dark as Homer inscribed the waves

and not like the glistening of iodine
on your Hart's lips with the grave
promise not delivered in Mixcoac.
No the sea was suicide

                        yellow on that day.

It seemed so beautiful, it seemed pure
radiance, all gold
                        as in a Turner canvas—
and on fire!

V 'WALKING ON THE MIRROR'

Their ship was the Orizaba, the sea,
the Caribbean. You can be sure Ivor
Winters never booked such a cruise,
that critic who slammed Crane for his
stale allusions to the sea, hardly guessed
Hart would literally drown in his own trope.

At midnight, alas, I had already missed
him, at midnight, he was no more alive
than when I first read his work and ventured
into the past, through this text, with language
as our only link, with language

81

as our talisman. Why is it that to find also
means to lose the grail. Irony of ironies. Holy of

holies, the bridegroom had been swept away
unwed with the ring buried in his pocket.
The figure into whose shadow I stepped
was the fiancée, his widow
in words. I watched her smoke away her left-
handed sorrow in the company of shrouded
lifeboats. Into the sea she flicked flaming ash
more brilliant than that star guiding the magi

millennia ago. Mary, you found not the man
but his wake. That winsome visage in the sea was
the moon not me, and Peg's lament was directed
to the reflection in her compact, to the pretty face
clouded with grief and powder. For a woman
the self must be portable in the purse and fulfill
the need to be made smaller by what she sees.
There was always too much woman in me and I
in none. Fancypants, flit, fetishist, fruit, faggot,
fairy, finocchio—That was me, all fay-male !

Did Peg tell you what our oh so sensitive
captain said about the likely manner of my
demise? 'If sharks didn't get the bloody
fool first then the propellers would have made
mincemeat of the body.' The body, the the
definite article, the object, not the man, not the
unrecoverable subject of this poem.

Christ could walk on water, but I believe,
not even He, without getting sucked
in, could have stepped on such a mirror,
a sea smooth as glass and as slippery,
the light at noon erasing all visible depth.

RILKE SENTIERO

Rose, oh reiner Widerspruch, Lust,
Niemandes Schlaf zu sein unter soviel
                    Lidern.

It's almost light when you stumble off the overnight train, the milkrun from the south, at the Montefalcone station. To drink in the dawn along with a spiced *caffe con latte* is sweet. You find a small café where it's easy to catch a fast cab for Duino where you unwind in the stillness of a village holding its breath. Moving into the 21st century, something slow! Something to surprise you with familiarity!

What? Your mecca is a mere suburb, 20 km from Trieste, a dormitory of geometric lawns, parallel streets, stucco walls and roses, roses

                                        opening reluctantly like
eyes after a deep and dreamless sleep, yes, fluttering petals like so many sticky eyelids over no eye. Cemetery comes from 'koimeterion', the Greek word for sleeping chamber, from 'koiman' meaning to put to sleep and this word is related to the Latin word, cunae, cradle. The poet here is an archaeologist of language. There are cities built on cities in each word. To dig is to unearth,
        to write is to excavate,
        to write is to discover.

        Like melody in music there is no meaning in the text
        without playing the words. Rilke, perpetually entering
        without arriving, concert tickets in his pockets, attuned

to the instrument he most feared 'because a person's life could be ruined if, even in passing, he happened to hear a violin, and that tone deflected his entire will to a denser fate.' He preferred, not music, but silence, its notation in the sea gull's cry, in the surge of surf, 'you see, I have not arrived at music yet, but I know about sounds.'

Such glossy charm! Duino offers you not a Northern Italian village, but a picture postcard for one. Duino, doo-eee-no, your name's a bird's call, doo-weee-know, your name's unanswerable.

Colours, though singularly bold in Italy, here seem demure, horticultural, not of the open field afire with wild poppies, but of plots, of containment. Those neatly fenced and hedged lawns are vivid evidence of how the Latin can so easily be tempered by the Teutonic. The expatriate from Canada empathizes. You too are hybrid—you too are hyphenated.

Longing for a nationalist identity is longing for stereotype! for simplification! How could you hope to find your true name in a flag, in the *tricolore* or the maple leaf? *ou les fleur de lis du Québec* ? Hybrid yes! Your species comes from the evolution of everything that lives by adding on. Hyphenated no! Hyphenated subtracts both ways, bears the sign of its division at the centre. Such is the insanity of the language of empty sign. Would you buy a carton with EGGS printed on it but with nothing inside? No? But the irony is if you're hungry you will pick it up even if you know that it's empty. It weighs less than nothing, but recalls for you the oily gold of yolk, the sun in a cloud of albumin.

Though you are just thinking of yourself and what you might eat for an American style breakfast, Rilke greets you. You feel rude for having read every one of his letters without writing back.

You think you understand why on his death bed Rilke refused an appointment to the German academy, how born in Bohemia, language failed to make him German enough. Though the angel spoke to him in *Deutsch*, Rilke sometimes wrote in French seeking what was the untranslatable poetic in himself. After all wasn't it the French, Rodin and Cezanne, who taught him how to look at things? Rilke lamented that through words it is too hard to get to the palpable world. In Paris he learned to pray differently, O for a palette thick with paint, O for the molten bronze of casting. Before the French he did not know how to see although he made do with vision. Before cubism he had to form himself entirely from the inside out.

In a letter to the Princess Maria, Rilke wrote that words were windows, 'not to the world, but to infinity', yes to infinity, to the intertextual in the Gutenberg galaxy.

There is also a poetry of no words, the poetry of the finite, of the mortal. Some read it in silence, not as when the concert ends though the body continues to vibrate with music, but as when the instrument, buried in its case, can't be touched. In this manner the dead compose most deeply. That recognition took longer than music to arrive. Rilke thought he was waiting to write in the way he could not wait for *La Benvenuta* to respond to his letters.

For every kiss you give me, darling, I'll give you three.

'It has always been my custom to write to you on this paper I normally use for working.' But for this stranger, for this most welcome one, for the woman who thanked him as her saviour, who said she knew him as a friend, although he did not know her, for *la Benvenuta* he used a higher element than onionskin. If his reach had not exceeded his grasp he would have skywritten her name with a comet.

La Benvenuta knew 'The Stories of God', she did not know the thin man in his fortieth year who was estranged from his wife and child. What he read in her letter was more than a reader's gratitude, her script echoed Beethoven's word, the same syllables Rilke imagined hearing from the lips of the Sphinx, *unpronounceable*, 'For you love music!'

To love a musician, a pianist, when you're tone deaf and unable to recall the simplest tune is natural if you love absence, if you love silence and the sounds which define it, if you love all those things which you are not. So it was not unnatural for Rilke to choose to court a woman whom he had never met, a woman who was already satisfied with him, who thanked him for a text written by a man he couldn't remember being. Did he hope that she could not be disappointed, she who already had what she wanted from him! And he—he was most happy in the writing to her!

But when writer met reader, he lost artistic control. When reader met writer she found him to be paler than his pages. And sadly the correspondence ended.

In the brochures the Italian, 'una passeggiata di sogno' is translated as 'a pleasant walk in the Castle gardens with light refreshments'. The morning moon is not the dreamer's, the morning moon only shines for those who do not sleep, for those who do not deign to eat. Rilke, this dawning, you are more wan than I ever imagined.

In its setting, the moon seems to pause over the solitary balcony facing out to sea where Rilke would practise listening. In thundering tempest listening, for the angel, for the *sotto voce*.

The cost of maintaining the prince's estate is raised through the sale of tickets for tours of the grounds and selected rooms. The royal secretary guides your group then offers you some tea, included in the price of admission. To think the prince raises his ordinary, if aristocratic, family here. Look, by the fountain, a child as thoughtless as your own has abandoned a golden ball.

In Firenze, during a visit to the Uffizi gallery, you entered a room crowded with other tourists. When Rilke saw the Sphinx, the crush of bodies made the monumental seem commonplace to him. You experienced something similar, something very different. The gallery did not empty suddenly, your eyes did. In the presence of the three graces all else was absence. Such brilliant light radiated from the painting you had to raise your hand to shield your eyes. Blinded by a Botticelli from the fifteenth century more alive than you are today.

The castle has the air of a church filled with invisible presence. 'Here is the angel, who doesn't exist, and the devil, who doesn't exist; and the human being, who does exist, stands between them, and (I can't help saying it) their unreality makes him more real to me.' More than any devil Rilke dreaded going home. In Clara's well-stocked cupboards, in rugs that needed beating, the visible world stalked. Chores made him feel unreal, ethereal. When a troublesome business letter found the scribe, even within the pristine portals of an Austrian dynasty, he was forced to deal with things, with accounts; his household goods were about to be auctioned off to pay the landlord in Paris. That day the sea clouded over of its own accord, that day he was numbed by numbers to its beauty, a sea silver with light, a north wind raging. 'Completely absorbed in the problem of how to answer the letter', he heard the angel of the elegies for the first time. He jotted down the angel's words in his notebook but ran inside to answer his creditor.

More than Lucifer himself Rilke feared distraction, interruption. Science offers a principle, a thermodynamic law, not a snake, not a woman, not her mate nor the little something they ate as the cause for death on Earth. Entropy curdled Rilke's dinner of fruit and milk. Was the anaemic poet right to desert his family and dedicate himself exclusively to the muse or to make the elegies, his greatest work, the property of Princess Marie von Thurn und Taxis-Hohenlohe, his hostess?

There was no way back from castle to cottage, no way home from royal mistress to wife, no way to hear the angel with his family, above the din, the quotidian. Or so he thought. While as royalty's guest he could enter the chapel with its invisible smells of incense and embalming fluids and feel more real than in the kitchen where Clara cooked every day another leek and potato soup.

Rilke's angel was not the guardian kind for children but the terrible mother of death and beauty. His art demanded no family but a sex with fatal edges, a sword, which would shine for him most brightly, but only in the distance, a brilliant blade to be kept sheathed.

In the castello di Duino several sabres, jewelled and orna-
mental are displayed under glass. Such danger is contained,
such danger is on show.

You like best the tower, its staircase, spiral, scalloped.
Some trade in their real body for an empty vessel where the
sea can sing more fully, more truly; some can only listen
from within the conch. At the centre of the vortex you
crouch. You are waiting for a sea change. Instead there is a
tapping on your shoulder, an official directing you to rejoin
the other tourists, all German except for the lone housewife
from Trieste, 'Sei, Italiana?'

Back to the present, back to sensuous delight, gardens
filled with roses. You can warm your hands by the red and
yellow blooms. But there are other hues which belong more
properly to the poet you admire. With the white and ghost-
ly blossoms strumming the trellis, you sense he would be
more deeply in tune.

O rose, many-petalled flower, flower feathered as if
winged, soaring seraphim of scent, it was you who killed
Rilke. By leukaemia, a rare blood disease, a septic infection
of the skin starting out from some slight wound. Dying
Rilke was comforted that his death was 'nobody's disease',
that it was his fate to succumb to a scratch from the thorn of
a rose tree.

In the body, memory has the power of smell. From each
garden and cottage gate, roses, their fragrance blaring all
the way down to the cliffs where the waves, weighty
enough to pound huge boulders into pebbles, fail to mute
that flower's scent.

Poor Rilke was a poet who learned to mine riches from
the unrequited; 'Don't think I'm wooing angel / and if I
were, you wouldn't come.' You seek to be trained in this art.
You have come to Duino to apprentice with even the stones
where he sometimes walked.

The elegies became the property of the princess. But his
silence may be shared by all, his silence is priceless.

Where you stroll along the marine drive, there's a Porsche,

there's an Alpha Romeo, there's a chameleon posing as a shrub. A man paints a wrought iron fence dark green. He rests on one knee as if he truly loves, as if he pleads to marry his job. It is not his fence, he's the hired man. Any stranger might guess from his frayed socks. Look where the back of his overalls ride up. This is not your garden, house, or estate for that matter, nor the palace for which you came in search of poetry, in search of his muse.

You discover a wooded path called Rilke Sentiero following the cliffs. Below on the beach, below on what must be some private shore, a single white bikini glows. Do you marvel to see the clothes when the woman's invisible?

What's mystery when it's all around you? Not home? Though the sun blazes now in a brilliant blue sky, you're still huddled in a raincoat with the collar rolled up. You ate some milk and fruit for supper almost a century ago. Hunger makes you light-headed.

No, Rilke never waited to write, he waited for dictation. Like a man sitting in the dark whose fingers grope for what withers in his pocket.

'Let such a person go out to his daily work, where/ greatness is lying in ambush.' What rooted, what stubborn Romanticism makes you still believe you won't understand Rilke unless it storms, you won't understand what shook him in the wake of this turquoise and

serene sea. Rilke in storm finding the Real,
Rilke in storm erecting a temple within the ear.